CHARLIE RED

Can Help

Inspired by the life of Dr. Charles R. Drew

by Sapphire Jule King

Illustrated by: Citlalin Morales

Level
K

For Cory,
My inspiration

NIKKI HOUSE BOOKS
An Imprint of Beacon Pinnacle Press

Dear Parent:

Our *Easy Next Step* books tell fictional stories inspired by real-life heroes of color. The same story is told with the same illustrations for reading levels K-3 using beginner sight words from each level. Now, your reader enters into a familiar world that will help him or her make progress with ease and meet the demands of the next level with less anxiety, fear, and frustration.

Follow the rating guide above and the word list, family discussion questions, and fun activities in the back to ignite your child's inner genius.

May each book fill your family with love and light.

Enjoy!

Sapphire Jule King, MAEd
Publisher | Reading Specialist

ISBN 978-0-9976878-1-1

Library of Congress Control Number: 2016909679

Library of Congress Subject Headings:
African Americans -- Juvenile fiction
History -- Juvenile fiction
Friendship -- Juvenile fiction
Self-reliance -- Juvenile fiction
Work -- Juvenile fiction
Problem Solving -- Juvenile fiction
Collaboration -- Juvenile fiction

Printed in the United States of America

Oh Father!
Oh Mother!

One red thing.

I want three.

Look, Charlie.

You can help.

7

See it go down.

Down, down, down.

I can do this.

I can not see.

The boy can
help me.

I can not help you.

Come jump, Charlie.

I can not.
You can help me.

We can make this.

See it go down.

We can make two.

Away we go.

See it go down.

See the boy.

See the
big red thing.

You can help me.

This can go here
and here.

Away we go.

27

Look Mother!
Look Father!

You are a
big help.

Social Studies Curriculum Standards and Topics

1. Understand the concept of the family
2. Understand what money is and why it is important
3. Understand goods and services
4. Understand needs and wants
5. Understand what makes a good citizen
6. Identify jobs people have

Family Discussion
Ask your child to retell the story to check for understanding. Then, ask the following questions for a deeper discussion:

1. What does Charlie want?
2. How does Charlie get more books?
3. What does Charlie do when he drops the newspapers?
4. Do all of the boys help Charlie?
5. What does Charlie do when one boy will not help?
6. How does Charlie feel when he sells all of the newspapers?

Help Charlie Red
Re-read this story aloud to your child. Ask how he or she would help Charlie Red sell his newspapers.

1. Can he or she think of a trick that Charlie Red could try?
2. Has he or she helped a parent or a friend before?

Have your child draw a picture or write a story in 20 words or less describing how they would help Charlie Red. Then, share it with us on Facebook, Instagram, or Twitter!

Fun Family Reading and Learning
Learn together as a family. Visit our website to view a list of other books about Dr. Drew and enjoy our fun, online games and learning activities.

Word List

Charlie Red Can Help uses the 35 words listed below.

Dolch Pre-primer Words

a	come	I	me	the
and	down	it	not	three
away	go	jump	one	two
big	help	look	red	we
can	here	make	see	you

Dolch Primer Words

are	do	this	want

Dolch Common Nouns   Higher Level Words

boy	Mother	Charlie	oh
Father	thing		

Spelling and Word Recognition Practice

1. Fold a piece of paper in half. Then, fold it in half again.
2. Cut the paper along the seams to make four squares.
3. Write one word along the top half of the paper square.
4. Have your child write the same word beneath your example.
5. Repeat this until all words are on a separate square of paper.
6. Use the squares as flashcards to help your child recognize and spell the words.

About the Author

Sapphire Jule King, MAEd

Sapphire Jule King's service to children in the US and abroad as an ESL teacher and developmental reading and math specialist spans more than 20 years. She holds a bachelor's degree in electrical engineering and a master's degree in adult education and training. Ms. King is President and CEO of Beacon Pinnacle Advisors LLC and Founding Chairman of the nonprofit International Freedom Coalition. She is a Houston native currenlty residing in Washington, D.C.

About the Illustrator

Citlalin "Star" Morales

Citlalin (si – klah – lin) Morales' interest in art started as a young child. She loved to wear bold, loud colors and carry markers and paper everywhere that she went. Her father named her after the Aztec word for "star" and an Aztec princess from folk stories. Ms. Morales is a first generation Mexican American with an associate degree in art. She is a Mississippi native and currently resides in Florida with her husband.

COMING SOON

Charlie Red Goes North:
Inspired by the life of Matthew Henson

Charlie Red Goes to School:
Inspired by the life of Dr. Carter G. Woodson

CPSIA information can be obtained
at www.ICGtesting.com
Printed in the USA
BVOW11s2300120716

455322BV00002B/2/P

9 780997 687811